OWJC

# WHAT CAN YOU DO WITH ONLY ONE SHOE?

# WHAT CAN YOU DO WITH ONLY ONE SHOE?

## Reuse, Recycle, Reinvent

## Simon and Sheryl Shapiro
## art by Francis Blake

**annick press**

toronto + new york + vancouver

We acknowledge the support of the Canada Council for the Arts, the Ontario Arts Council, and the Government of Canada through the Canada Book Fund (CBF) for our publishing activities.

Cataloging in Publication

Shapiro, Simon, author
    What can you do with only one shoe? : reuse, recycle, reinvent / Simon and Sheryl Shapiro ; art by Francis Blake.

ISBN 978-1-55451-643-8 (bound).--ISBN 978-1-55451-642-1 (pbk.)

    1. Children's poetry, Canadian (English). I. Shapiro, Sheryl, author II. Blake, Francis, illustrator III. Title.

PS8637.H368W53 2014        jC811'.6        C2013-906702-7


Distributed in Canada by:
Firefly Books Ltd.
50 Staples Avenue, Unit 1
Richmond Hill, ON  L4B 0A7

Published in the U.S.A. by Annick Press (U.S) Ltd.
Distributed in the U.S.A. by:
Firefly Books (U.S.) Inc.
P.O. Box 1338
Ellicott Station
Buffalo, NY  14205

Printed in China

Visit us at: www.annickpress.com
Visit Francis Blake at: www.francisblake.com


Also available in e-book format.
Please visit www.annickpress.com/ebooks.html for more details. Or scan

Jarvis Bob & Polly

# THE PLANTER

Someone just gave me a planter.
She got it from I-don't-know-where.
I must say the shape is peculiar.
I must say I really don't care.

I'll plant it with flowers that start with a P,
which seems an appropriate letter.
With purple petunias and pansies and phlox,
I can't think of anything better.

But if I get tired of these plants, version one,
I'm certain of what I will do.
I'll simply reach out
and I'll flush them away,
and replace them with
plants number two.

# ONE SHOE

What can you do
with only one shoe?
You can hop, hop along
'til the sole wears right through.

You can wear it on top
of your head like a hat.
You could use it to make sure
your pancake is flat.

You could cook it and eat it
–a leathery steak–
though you might end up getting
a big stomach ache.

But the silliest,
uselessest thing–you'd agree–
is to nail that lonely old
shoe to a tree.

# HOW MANY FISH DOES
# IT TAKE TO CHANGE
# A LIGHT BULB?

Only one
lonely one.
Waiting 'til
the cleaning's done.

# THE BOAT'S COMPLAINT

If you think that it's fun just to
float as a boat–
it is not!

You get hot, you get cold.
You get wet, you get mold.
You get rot, you get old.

Sometimes it's quite dull
'til you're bombed by a gull
and you find you have bird
doo-doo right on your hull!

Sometimes there's a gale
that can rip off your sail.
Or your deck can be smashed
by the tail of a whale.

So you're hoping one day
that you'll be far away
from the fish and the smell
of the sea and the spray.
Yay! Your seat will be dry
at the end of the day.

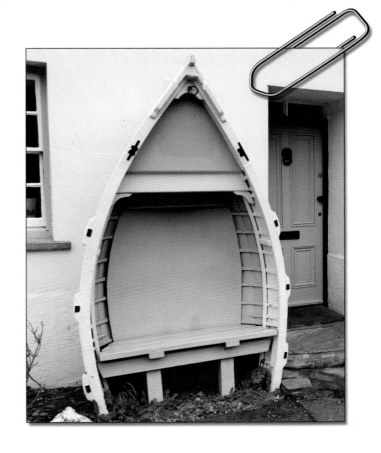

# THE PICNIC

If you're wanting to picnic on uneven ground,
where your table's unstable or up on a mound,
stop and think! Be creative! The answer's around.

It isn't a knife and it isn't a spoon—
but the food's coming out so we need it real soon.

It isn't a shovel, it isn't a pick—
but we're all getting hungry, so think of it—quick.

And you do, just in time for the meal to begin.
It's a fork—here's the food—we can start. Dig right in!

# MAKING MUSIC

One can, two can. Who can? You can!
Using junk from the landfill site.
Rusty cans and wood and wire,
thrumming, strumming, day and night.

# DREAM CAR

It's a bed like no other,
a wonderful sight.
The body is red.
The upholstery is white.

You climb into bed
when you run out of steam.
As your head hits the pillow
you're off in a dream.

You speed down a highway,
the wind in your face,
and your friends can't believe
just how fast you can race.

You drive through the night,
moon and stars overhead.
When you wake up at dawn
you're still snuggled in bed.

# SUPERMARKET BUGGY RAP

One push–and *whoosh*!
You zoom a mile along the aisle.
Shoppers stare at flying hair
and you don't care.

The cart was new
but now it's not!

Now ...
you really hate
that it won't run straight
and the wheels all grate.
It's done.
It's done with the groceries,
with the mac and cheese,
with the cookies and teas,
and the cans of peas.
It's done.
It's no more fun.

Give it a cushion, green paint, four feet;
no more pushin', a cart it ain't, now it's a seat.

## RE-TIRED

A farmer knew *just* what to do
when his cow was too thirsty to moo.
His solution was thrifty–
"repurposing"–nifty!
Which saves the environment, too.

# RECYCLE

I recycled my bike
and created a dog,
from the chain and the pedals
and saddle and cog.

He's a dog that won't bite
or annoy with a bark.
He will never chase cats
or get lost in the park.

Mom and Dad love him.
There's no need for vets.
He can live in our condo
that won't allow pets.

He's almost perfection
from tail to toes.
It's really a shame
that he can't lick my nose.

# STREET SWEEPER

*One broom by hand*
*was oh-so-slow.*
*Invention is*
*the way to go!*

Tractor driver,
clever feller.
At his back
a broom propeller.

Whirling, sweeping,
what a sight!
Pebbles flying
left and right.

He can zoom.
He can brake.
No one wants
to overtake!

# PLAYGROUND AMBULANCE

Emergency! We need equipment.
Gotta have a swing and slide.
Gotta have some bars to climb on.
Gotta have a place to hide.

Bring it in with sirens blaring.
I know how to get it done.
It will be here in one minute,
just by calling 9-1-1.

# I REALLY LOVE ...

I really loved my blue jeans
and they fit me perfectly.
So I wore them 'til the denim
disappeared, first at the knee.

Then the thigh.
And the calf.
And the bottoms were kind of ragged, too.

Then Mom said that my favorite jeans
must go 'cos they're worn through.
I begged—she wouldn't listen
because parents never do.

So I snuck away the blue jeans
and it could have been much worse.
I made some alterations.
Now I really love my purse.

## PHOTO CREDITS